KARMA IS THREE CATS

Life According to Taylor Swift's Kitty Best Friends

I0813787

Bella Montgomery
Illustrated by Carolina Marando

mudpuppy

We're Meredith Grey,
Olivia Benson, and
Benjamin Button—
three of the hardest-working
kitties in show business.

ALL BY DESIGN...

We spend our days helping our famous mom, Taylor, be a musical mastermind.

DAY
A
HAIRYTALE

Being her muse is a big job.
It's purring in her lap
because we love her.

But it's also. . .

. . . causing a little trouble
to keep her on her paws.

... TROUBLE ...
ERAS
ME!

It's long days of shooting. But that's show business, baby. We're living our wildest dreams.

Lights, camera, CATion!

We're her purrsonal stylists, making sure she shimmers when she walks into a room.

DEFINITELY

When she has a big choice to make, we're her loyal kitty committee.
DON'T CARE
WHAT?

We go everywhere she goes because she knows we belong with her.

Doctor
Meredith
Grey

After all, someone has to remind her to stretch before her shows . . .

OR SWIFT
rasTour
TAYL

. . . and help her calm down when she's finished for the night.

Calm Down

We watch her blue eyes shine
when she's happy and let her
steal kisses when she's feeling down.

Then she shakes it off, gets right back on her white horse, and shows us what she's made of.

SMILE
STAY
FEAR
TOO
ALL
ME
AUGUST

She weaves clever clues to untangle, but where do you think she got the string? We know all too well!

She tells us how much
she adores her fans,
so we make sure to
show our love, too.

The best part of our job is bringing her joy so she can sing and sparkle with you.

This is the story of us—
her best friends and
kitty crew, for meow,
forever, and always.

KARMA IS THREE CATS. © 2024 Castle Point Publishing
All rights reserved. No portion of this book may be reproduced or transmitted in any form or by any means, electronic or mechanical, including photocopying, recording, and other information storage and retrieval systems, without prior written permission of the publisher.

mudpuppy

www.mudpuppy.com • @mudpuppykids
70 West 36th Street
New York, NY 10018

Special thanks to Diann Calvert

Illustrations by Carolina Marando
Editorial by Jennifer Calvert & Monica Sweeney
Design by Katie Jennings Campbell

ISBN: 978-0-7353-8529-0

First Edition: 2024
Designed and printed in the United States of America.
10 9 8 7 6 5 4 3 2 1

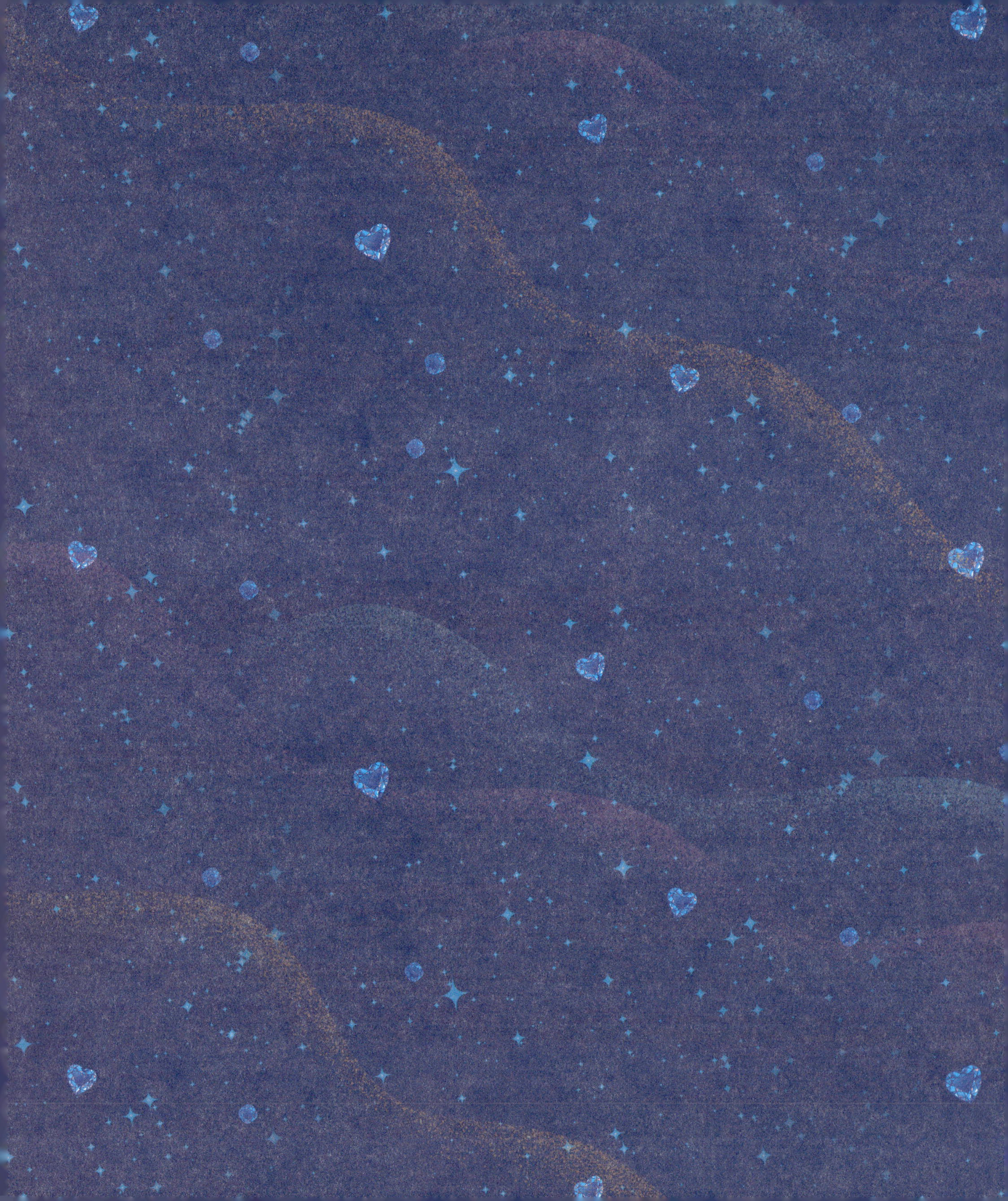